D0524406

Audrey Hepburn.

The 101 DALMATIANS

WALT DISNEY PRODUCTIONS

HIPPO BOOKS
Scholastic Book Services
London

Scholastic Book Services Inc.
10 Earlham Street, London WC2H 9LN

Scholastic Inc.
730 Broadway, New York, NY 10003, USA

Scholastic Tab Publications Ltd.
123 Newkirk Road, Richmond Hill, Ontario L4C 3G5,
Canada

Ashton Scholastic, Box 579,
Gosford, New South Wales, Australia

Ashton Scholastic Ltd,
165 Marua Road, Panmure, Auckland, New Zealand

All rights reserved
Made and Printed in Spain by Mateu Cromo, Madrid
Reprinted 1985

Copyright © 1984 Walt Disney Productions
Worldwide rights reserved
This edition first published 1984 by Scholastic Book Services, Inc.
10 Earlham Street, London WC2H 9LN by arrangement with
Walt Disney Productions.

This book is sold subject to the condition that it shall not, by way of trade or otherwise
be lent, resold, hired out, or otherwise circulated without the publisher's prior
consent in any form of binding or cover other than that in which it is published and
without a similar condition, including this condition, being imposed upon the
subsequent purchaser.

Roger Radcliffe and Pongo, his
dalmatian, met Anita and
Perdita, her dalmatian, in the
park. When Roger and Anita
got married Pongo and Perdita
were delighted.

Within a few months Pongo and Perdita were expecting puppies.
Roger and Anita were thrilled, so was Anita's friend Cruella de Vil.
She wanted a coat made of black-and-white spotted fur, and kept
on asking Roger if he would sell all the puppies to her. Pongo and
Perdita were very frightened of her, and worried about what would
happen to their puppies.

When the puppies were born Nanny brought one to show to Pongo and Roger. Perdita had fifteen puppies altogether, and Nanny made a comfortable bed for them in the kitchen.

They were beautiful puppies and soon began to grow. Cruella used to telephone Anita to see how they were doing, but Roger refused to sell any of them to her no matter what she offered him.

One winter evening Roger and Anita took Pongo and Perdita for a walk, leaving Nanny in charge of the puppies. She was very suspicious of the two men from the electric company who came to the front door, but they forced their way into the house. They tricked her into leaving the kitchen, and when she came back the puppies were gone.

Roger and Anita were in despair. They called the police, the newspapers, anyone they thought would help, but nothing was heard of the stolen puppies. (Cruella was delighted when she read the news.) "It's up to us, Perdita," said Pongo, and that evening in the park he barked the whole story to the twilight barking (this is the dog's way of passing on news). His story was heard by dogs all over London, and quickly travelled throughout the country.

It was picked up by an intelligent bloodhound in Suffolk. "The colonel must be told about this," he said to himself, "he'll know what to do." He barked the story as loudly as possible, for the

colonel was a little deaf. But his able sergeant Tibs had very good hearing indeed, and made sure the colonel understood the importance of the message.

Sergeant Tibs also told the colonel about the peculiar goings on next door at Hell Hall. "Well done, Tibs," said the colonel. "We'd better go and investigate."

When Sergeant Tibs slunk into the house, an extraordinary sight met his eyes. There were hundreds (or so it seemed) of small dalmatian puppies all watching television, watched over by two men, Saul and Jaspar Baddum. (The men looked very like the two strange characters from the electric company – though Tibs didn't know this!).

Tibs hurried back to the colonel who asked the twilight barking to pass on a message to Pongo and Perdita that the puppies had been found. He then asked Tibs to go back and keep watch to see what happened next.

Pongo and Perdita set out immediately they heard the news. It was very cold and snowy, but the dogs in the twilight barking chain made sure they got to Suffolk as quickly and safely as they could.

As they drew near to Hell Hall an enormous car, with Cruella de Vil at the wheel, roared past them and disappeared through the gates.

Cruella de Vil burst into the room where Jaspar and Saul were watching the puppies. She demanded that they produce ninety-nine black-and-white spotted furs by the time she arrived back that evening or else. . .

Sergeant Tibs had to help the puppies to escape. They were delighted to see him, for they felt something unpleasant was about to happen to them.

The puppies poured through a hole in the wall watched over by
Tibs. When Pongo and Perdita arrived to help their puppies were
very excited to see them again.

Suddenly Jaspar and Saul realized what was happening. They set off in search of the puppies, but they reckoned without Pongo and Perdita, who took care of them in no uncertain way.

As soon as all the puppies were outside Pongo took charge. "Hurry," he said, "we must find somewhere safe to stop, because they will be on our trail soon." He brushed over their tracks in the snow with the branch of a tree. They were tired and hungry but he knew Cruella would not give up until she found them. They had to get back to Roger and Anita.

At one village on the way they met a friendly black labrador who had heard about their flight. He told them about an old bakery where they could hide. "And I think I have found a way to get you back to London. There's a van loading up outside, and there's room for all of you."

There was a screeching of brakes as Cruella's car stopped outside the bakery, followed by Saul and Jaspar in their van. "Search everywhere," she stormed. "They cannot be far away."

Whenever they had the chance, Pongo, Perdita and the black labrador scurried across the road with as many puppies as they could and loaded them into the van. But the puppies black-and-white coats showed up brilliantly in the darkness. Two of the puppies started fighting in the fireplace, which was full of soot. "That's the answer", cried Pongo. "Everybody roll in the soot. Cruella de Vil isn't looking for black dogs!"

Cruella didn't notice the black puppies pouring into the van until a drop of melting snow made white spots appear on the backs of Pongo and the last two puppies as they scrambled hastily aboard and the van set off for London.

"That was them," Cruella yelled. She pointed to Jaspar and Saul. "Follow that van. You take the other road and together we'll cut it off," she cried.

But Jaspar and Saul, hopelessly out of control, crashed into Cruella's car at the foot of the hill, while the van went happily on its way to London.

Anita couldn't believe her eyes when a large black dog jumped on her lap, and she looked at the enormous number of puppies! But as Nanny brushed off the soot she recognized Perdita and Pongo and their own puppies as well as eighty-four others! "We'll keep all one hundred and one" cried Roger. "We'll move to a house in the country and have a dalmatian plantation!"